THE
NIGHT
BEFORE
CHRISTMAS
IN
CALIFORNIA

Text
Catherine Smith

Illustrations
Steve Egan

ISBN 0-87905-487-5
prpk 10: 0-87905-540-5
prpk 20: 0-87905-499-9
This is a Peregrine
Smith book, published by
Gibbs Smith, Publisher
P.O. Box 667
Layton, Utah 84041

First edition
95 94 93 92 5 4 3 2 1
Copyright © 1992
by Gibbs Smith, Publisher

On the night

before

Christmas,

all down 101

The traffic was

deadlocked;

it wasn't

much fun.

The parties

were starting;

the hosts in

despair;

In hope

that the

catered food

soon would

be there.

The fine

salad greens

and the aged

Chardonnay

Were stalled on

the freeways

and there they

might stay.

The salesfolk

at Broadway

were glancing

at clocks

While last

minute

shoppers

seized sweaters

and socks,

To fill

stockings

hung by

the chimney

with care,

In hopes that

good St. Nick

would

somehow get

there.

The sky over

Tahoe was

starry and

bright,

But the fog

on the coast

would last all

through the night.

As KNX

broadcast

the news of

the hour,

The picture

looked bleak

and the outlook

was dour.

From far

Crescent City

the story was

flashed:

"St. Nick and the

reindeer

have possibly

crashed –

"The fog

is so thick even

Rudolph

can't lead

"And Santa

has said,

'It's a problem

indeed.

"'My fog lights

are powerful,

but this is

pea soup.

"'The poor reindeer

can't make

their way through

such goop.'"

Into 10 million

homes

came this

horrible news.

There was

wonder in Fresno,

shock in

Santa Cruz.

"Let's form an

initiative,

Proposition C,

"Let's ban

fog on

Christmas Eve;

it just can't be."

The children

were up;

they would not

go to bed

They were

watching TV,

and they heard

what was said.

They thought

of the stockings

they'd hung

up with care

Hanging limp

and unfilled,

with no presents

to share.

They thought

of the

10 million toys

gathering dust,

Piled up

at the North Pole

and starting

to rust.

And all through

the suburbs

arose

such a clamor

It rang through

the night

like a screaming

jackhammer.

The governor

was called

and the mayors

alerted.

The need

for solutions

was loudly

asserted.

They called

on the Warriors;

they called

on the Lakers;

The Giants,

Rams, Clippers . . .

but there were

no takers.

The night

hours were passing

and Santa

was groaning

He still had to do

Idaho

and Wyoming.

When finally

a lawyer

in south

Contra Costa

Sprang up

from her dinner

of angel hair

pasta:

"I'll get a

court order,

a clean writ

of habeas.

"We'll outlaw

this fog,

send it off to

Las Vegas."

The forces

were mustered,

the deed

quickly done,

And Santa

completed

his rounds

on a run.

The children

were cheering,

the parents

ecstatic,

The palm trees

were swaying,

the vistas

dramatic.

From Southland

to Napa,

Sierras

to coast,

Came a message

from Santa,

more grateful

than most.

It swept

through the

Golden State,

ringing

and bright,

"Merry Christmas

to all

and to all

a Good Night."